Welcome to
Eggbert's Adventures.
Written in consultation
with parents, teachers and
the children themselves,
this book aims to widen children's
vocabulary and hone their
reading ability, whilst
providing great enjoyment,
entertainment and
education.

Paul Gustafson

OXFORD

Eggbert's Adventures
at the Fair

Paul Gustafson
Illustrated by Ray Mutimer

Eggbert wakes up, he's had sweet dreams,
Of koalas and hippos and silver moonbeams.

Mum calls to Eggbert, "Come on down.
You'll be glad to hear that the fair is in town."

He looks out of his window and, to his surprise,
Sees a whole new adventure in front of his eyes.

Dad opens the door and shouts, "Hello!
Grab your coats, it's time to go."

They walk out of the gate towards the fair.
The sound of music and laughter is everywhere.

"Oh, look!" says Eggbert. "Shelley's over there.
Can I walk with her around the fair?"

"Yes," says Dad, "but please beware,
Some rides can be frightening - like that one there!"

Into the tunnel the two friends go,
And see the ghosts all aglow.

Skeletons and spiders with long hairy legs,
Bats and beetles and large dusty webs.

The Bad Eggs jump out and give them a fright,
Eggbert and Shelley have both turned white!

The Bad Eggs laugh. They like being mean.
But when a ghost jumps out they tremble and scream.

PC Capon says, "It serves you right.
You were wrong to give Eggbert and Shelley a fright."

Shelley asks Eggbert, "Can we play that game?
We can win a koala if we guess the right name."

Eggbert's eyes open, he could get his wish.
Three balls in the bucket to win a goldfish.

He hands over his money and gets five balls to throw.
The first two are in. "Go, Eggbert! Go!"

The third and fourth are out by a mile.
The fifth one bounces, but makes Eggbert smile.

Shelley and Eggbert both get their wish.
She gets her koala and he gets his fish.

The two little friends walk back through the fair. "Look," says Shelley, "at what's over there."

"Yum, yum!" says Eggbert. "There's fish and chips, Candyfloss, toffee apples and sherbet dips."

Eggbert and Shelley meet Mum and Dad.
What a wonderful time at the fair they've all had.

Eggbert says, "Dad, look what I've found.
This purse was lying there on the ground."

Dad tells Eggbert, "You must hand it in.
I've always taught you to do the right thing."

PC Capon asks, "What have we here?
Is this the purse you have lost, my dear?"

The lady says, "Thank you! I'll give you a treat.
This is my ride, so please take a seat."

The Twister starts slowly, then gets very quick.
The Bad Eggs are dizzy and feeling quite sick.

Eggbert and Shelley step off the ride.
The Bad Eggs are swaying from side to side.

At the end of a day that was full of surprises,
Eggbert and Shelley go home with their prizes.

Mum and Dad kiss Eggbert, "Goodnight."
Then walk to the door and turn out the light.

The fish in his bowl and Eggbert in bed.
The thoughts of the day spin round in his head.

TM

For Mathew

The author would like to thank
Kerri Bracey, Jim Moore, Peta Lloyd and Doug Califano
in the preparation of this book.

Eggsact Books Ltd, 30 Bankside Court, Stationfields, Kidlington, Oxford OX5 1JE.
Distribution: John (Booksellers) Limited, The Old School, First Turn, Wolvercote, Oxford OX2 8BP.
Telephone: (01865) 512424. Fax: (01865) 311434.
www.eggbertsadventures.co.uk

ISBN 0-9542972-3-7

First published 2004.

Printed by and bound in Europe by Colours Commercial Print, Oxford.

The right of Paul Gustafson and Ray Mutimer to be identified
as the author and illustrator of this work respectively has been asserted
by them in accordance with the Copyright, Designs and Patents Act, 1988.